This book is given with love to...

·THE·
SECRET
WORDS

by

Dominic Anglim

illustrations

Marta Magnuska

Once upon a time,
there lived an Aye-aye
called Rija.

Rija lived with her mum, dad, her older
brother Tojo, and her younger sister Avana,
high up in a canopy tree, on the island of
Madagascar.

During the daytime, she slept in her nest
with her family, and at night she helped her
mum find food in the trees.

Rija liked finding fruit on the low branches the best,
because whenever she started to climb higher,
she thought,

"I can't do it"

and couldn't climb any higher.

So she stayed on the lower branches,
where the fruit grew close to their nest.

Tojo and his friends always played on
the higher branches, they would climb
so high up and all Rija could do
was watch from below.

She wanted to climb up to them, but again,
whenever she tried, she would think
the same thing,

"I can't do it!"

In school, Rija was a good student. She liked to read and write. But whenever there was a test, she got nervous and thought,

"I can't do it!"

So she never got the good grades she wanted.

I can't do it !

Rija played tennis and even though she did have fun playing, she never managed to win a game. Because when she was playing, she would think,

"I can't do it!"

And she'd miss every ball!

Avana was
just learning to climb now.
She could climb much higher
than Rija ever could.

One night, Avana was playing with Tojo
and his friends when suddenly she fell!
She was much higher than Rija had ever
been and now she needed help, fast.
Rija looked up and heard Avana call out,

"Rija! Help!"

Tojo was too far away to make it in time.
But then, something new happened,
Rija said to herself,

"I can do this!"

And she leaped up to a branch
that was below where Avana was falling...
and caught her before she hit the ground!

Tojo arrived seconds later,
"Rija! That was amazing!"

"I've never seen you jump that far before!
How did you do that?!"

Rija thought back to right before she jumped.
That's when she remembered what she had
thought,

"I told myself, I can do this
and I jumped!"

"Wow that was so brave" said Tojo.

Avana had already started climbing again but this time she was climbing down to their nest.

The next night, at school, there was a test and Rija felt different than normal. When the test started, she waited for a moment, closed her eyes and thought to herself,

"I can do this!"

and then she began to write.

At the end of class, Mrs. Rova called her over "Rija, this is the best score you've ever gotten! You must have prepared a lot for this test!"

"I did, but it was more than that Mrs. Rova. Before I started, I told myself, I can do this and then started writing!"

"That's fantastic Rija! You know, those words
are secret words that not many people know!
Telling yourself you can do something
is very powerful.

And even if you don't succeed the first time, you
can always repeat and succeed the next. In fact,
the only way to succeed at anything in life
is by trying and learning through failure!"

The next night, Rija was playing a tennis match and right before she served, she told herself her secret words,

"I can do this!"

And you know what?
She won her first ever game!

From that day onwards, Rija started to always use her secret words for everything she did.

And even if she didn't succeed straight away, she didn't mind, because now, she told herself,

"I can do this, if not tonight, then the next night, or the one after that!"

The End

Claim your FREE Gift!

 Visit:

PDICBooks.com/Gift

Thank you for purchasing
The Secret Words

and welcome to the Puppy Dogs & Ice Cream family.
We're certain you're going to love the little gift
we've prepared for you at the website above.

9 781953 177018

CPSIA information can be obtained
at www.ICGtesting.com
Printed in the USA
BVHW022107300621
610841BV00001B/6